NEW YEAR, KNEW YOU

CAPRICORN COVE SERIES

EVIE MITCHELL

THUNDER THIGHS PUBLISHING

ACKNOWLEDGEMENT OF COUNTRY

I acknowledge the Traditional Custodians of the lands on which I write, the Ngunnawal people, and pay my respect to elders both past and present.

I acknowledge the continued and deep spiritual relationship of the Australian Aboriginal and Torres Strait Islander peoples' to this land, and their unique cultural and spiritual relationships to the land, waters and seas and their rich contribution to society.

Always was, always will be.

To those struggling to love themselves.
You are strong. You are beautiful.
Put on your crown, hold up your sword, you rule
your own kingdom.
Don't let anyone take that power away from you —
especially yourself.

And to my husband,
Thank you for teaching me that it's okay to love
myself.
You make me feel sexy even when I'm in fluorescent
lighting on the first day of my period, cloaked in a
potato sack.

Though, to be fair, you rarely force me to wear the
sack anymore...

NEW YEAR KNEW YOU

Emily

The doctors told me I have amnesia. They've said it's a result of the concussion I sustained on New Year's Eve, but I know the truth.

I've been transported to a parallel universe. It's the only plausible explanation as to why I'm now living five years in the future, where I've morphed into some kind of crazy bully who has a better relationship with my mother-in-law than my husband.

Or should I say, ex-husband? How is it that Calvin Jameson and I have gone from hopelessly devoted to separated and on the cusp of divorce?

I can't remember, but I'm damned sure I'm going to find out.

Calvin

I love my wife. The problem is, I no longer like her. After our wedding, she morphed from the dorky barefooted hippy into a prim and proper Stepford wife whose tongue is sharper than a sword.

When Emily wakes up from a coma claiming not to remember the last five years – I'm sceptical. But then she shows signs of the old her. The woman who eats burgers with extra fries, who wants to learn how to juggle, who plays the violin naked and dreams of exploring every beach the world has to offer.

And I have to ask myself – what if I just ignore the last five years? What if this is our do-over?

Warning: This new year love story involves a woman searching for redemption, a man who's been burned before, and the magic that only a new year brings. This second-chance love will tug on your heartstrings, remind you to love yourself and literally burn your sheets – sometimes all in the same chapter! Get thee some tissues and a hot man to cuddle, this is going to be one angsty ride.

Trigger warning: This book deals with body issues, bullying, and self-confidence. If this is a trigger for you, please consider skipping.

CHAPTER 1

Emily

I don't remember buying a new alarm clock. Or getting drunk last night. I have to assume the two are related – it's the only explanation for the incessant pounding in my head.

Keeping my eyes closed, I reached out, blindly feeling for the alarm, my arm feeling strangely weak and weighted. Instead of the wooden side table that sat beside my bed, my fingertips encountered cool, sleek metal.

I frowned, attempting to force my heavy eyes open. My success was limited as I snapped them shut, wincing at the stabbing pain the light shot through my eyes into the depth of my brain.

Am... am I dead?

No, you ninny, no one feeling this level of pain could be dead.

I pried one eye open, then the other, blinking and squinting as I took in the unfamiliar room. White walls and grey floors with tubes and wires that ran from beeping machines to me.

I blinked.

Shit. Is this... a hospital?

A nurse hovered at my side.

"Emily? Emily, can you hear me?"

I lifted a hand, moving with a slow lethargy as I reached up to touch my face.

Definitely not dead.

My fingers traced dressings stuck to my forehead, and as I explored the dress. Their size surprised me, as did the pain that arched through my skull as I grazed my fingers across the bandage.

The nurse reached for my hand, pulling it away from my head as she continued to ask if I could hear her.

I swallowed, nausea swirling in my stomach.

What happened?

"I can hear you," I tried to say, but the words sounded both muffled and jumbled as they left my mouth.

"Welcome back,'" the nurse smiled,

reaching over my head. I heard a buzzer go off as she withdrew. "I'm just calling the doctor, and we'll get you all checked over."

"Where's Cal?" I tried to ask, feeling my mouth struggling to form words.

"Just rest for a minute, Emily. Let your body adjust."

I closed my eyes, a distressed whimper sneaking up my throat. Between the lights, the sounds and the constant throbbing, stabbing pain in my head, I had no idea how to cope with this level of sensory overload.

"Mrs. Jameson? I'm Doctor Jenkins. Can you open your eyes for me?"

Cal's mother is here? Oh no!

I forced my lids open, immediately shuttering them against the light, then reopening them at half-mast.

"Good." He had a kindly face, grey hair, and more wrinkles than I expected for a man of his age. "I'm just going to check you over. Can you tell me your name?"

"Emily Knight," I whispered, the words slightly more audible.

He paused in the act of reaching for my hand.

"Knight?" he repeated.

I tried to nod, the reaction instinctive. Pain shot through my head, my world shifting, my vision blurring. I snapped my eyes closed, my world continuing to spin as I struggled to suck in air, trying desperately to suppress the nausea swirling in the pits of my stomach.

The machine beside me buzzed, blaring out an ear-piercing trill.

I felt the doctor shift beside me, and a moment later, the machine stopped buzzing. He moved down the bed, placing his hands on the soles of my feet.

"Okay, Emily. Can you push against my hands?"

I pushed, feeling weak but grateful for his approving sounds.

"Good." He let my feet go, moving up my body as he checked for movement. "Can you tell me what day it is?"

"New Year's Eve," I whispered, eyes still shuttered.

"Close but not quite. Your accident happened two days ago. You've been in a coma since then." He touched my neck, feeling around the back and asking if anything hurt.

The muscles were sore, whiplash perhaps? But I didn't feel overwhelming pain like that in my head.

"What happened?"

"Do you know what year it is?"

"If it's the new year, then it has to be twenty-fifteen."

The doctor's hand rested on my shoulder.

"Twenty-fifteen?" he clarified.

"Mm."

"What's the last thing you remember?" he asked, his tone soothing, his voice quiet.

I wracked my brain, desperate to remember. "A party. Cal, my fiancé, was there. We were driving home." I shot up, trying to focus on one of the two doctors weaving before me. "Where's Cal?"

Double vision. Nausea. Pain. Bandages. We've been in an accident. Shit. Shit. Shit! Where's Cal?

"Your hus—fiancé is fine. He wasn't involved in the crash. He's just popped home to get a change of clothes, but we'll advise him of your waking and ensure he returns soon."

I closed my eyes, embracing the dark. "Okay. What happened?"

"Your car came off the road and hit a tree. Emily, I need you to open your eyes so I can do some tests. Can you do that for me?"

The tests were straightforward but left me exhausted and in more pain.

"Right, we're going to get you some more pain medication. You'll likely sleep after it's administered. That's for the best right now. The double vision is to be expected but should wear off in the next day or so. We're going to run a few more tests, but I'll talk about them after you rest."

"Okay," I muttered, eyes squeezed tight against the bright lights.

"We'll also move you out of ICU to a ward. Your vitals look good, though this concussion is nasty. You've received a few minor abrasions and have some rather painful bruising, but overall you're lucky it's not worse."

I tried to ask what happened, tried to form the words with my exhausted mouth. But the painkillers were flowing through my system, and the pull of blissfully painless sleep called.

I sank down into the nothingness, embracing the dark.

I NEXT WOKE in a different room with a slightly less painful head. This room had dim lighting and fewer machines. My sister sat with her husband in chairs beside the window, quietly murmuring.

"Collins?" my whisper was nothing more than a hoarse exhalation of air.

"Oh, Emily." Collins surged forward, immediately disengaging from Nick to come to my side, her fingers intertwining with mine. "You're awake. Thank God!"

"How long?" I asked, the words struggling to make it past the dry desert of my mouth.

"Just another few hours."

Nick rose. "I'll get the nurse."

"Cal?" I asked, noting yet again his absence. Fear and anxiety warred in my stomach, a bitter brewing mess. They weren't telling me something.

Collins soothed a hand over my head, brushing back stray hairs. I tried not to wince at the waves of pain that action sent through my body.

"You still have exceptionally poor timing. I sent him to get a coffee. He'll be back any minute."

"He's okay?"

"Em, you were the only one injured."

I closed my eyes, letting myself sink back on the bed, relief turning my bones to liquid.

I heard steps; those footfalls as familiar to me as the back of my hand.

"Cal."

And like a welcome rain after a drought, he appeared big, broad and looking as if his face were carved with worry and exhaustion.

And a beard.

When did he grow a beard?

A fission of something unfamiliar and ugly raced down my back, finding a home in my stomach.

"Emily." He strode immediately to my bed, handing off the coffee cup in his hand to Collins as he dropped into the vacant seat at the side of my bed, his hand immediately reaching to mine, removing it from Collins' grasp and pressing his palm to my own. "You're awake."

I tried to nod, immediately gritting my teeth against the searing pain pounding through my head. "Are you okay?"

"Of course," he replied immediately, pressing a kiss to the back of my hand. "You were the only one in the car."

"I don't remember."

He shook his head. "It doesn't matter. All that matters is that you're okay."

I tried to squeeze his hand but could only manage a limp flex of my fingers. "I love you."

"Love you too, Pretty Eyes. And I'm sorry. I want you to give me another chance."

Another chance?

"What?"

He rose, pressing a chaste kiss to my lips. His beard scratched my face in a way that felt unfamiliar. I reached up, brushing a finger over the hair, a rasping sound following my movement.

"When did you grow this? How long have I been out?"

The room went electric. Cal's eyes darkened, a frown marking his brow.

"Emily," he said slowly. "What do you mean? I've had this beard for two years."

I scoffed, rolling my eyes and finding it was yet another movement I couldn't do with a head injury.

"Ow," I reached up, gingerly touching my temple. "Stop joking around. Everything hurts."

"Em... I'm not joking. I've had this for at least two years." Cal's grip tightened on my hand. "Baby, what day is it?"

"I... they said it was after new year's, so maybe the third or something?"

"But what year?" Collins asked from beside Cal, her face pale.

"Twenty-fifteen."

Cal collapsed into a vacant chair, shoving fingers into his hair. Beside him, Collins gasped, covering her mouth, her eyes wide as she stared at me.

"What? You guys are scaring me."

"Baby," Cal whispered, his voice rough. "It's twenty-twenty."

Nick and a nurse chose that moment to enter the room.

"Mrs—er, that is—Emily!" The nurse said

brightly, walking immediately to the bed. "The doctor is on his way. Let me just check you over."

She began the tests, fussing with my blankets and asking me questions as I tried to process her reactions.

It was as she lifted my hand that I realised something.

"Wait," I said, pulling my wrist away from her and holding it up to my face. I stared at the faded tattoo on my wrist, unable to remember when I'd sat for the artwork.

This isn't my hand.

Panic ballooned in my chest, my heart crashing against my rib change as my stomach took a dive.

This isn't my hand!

I thrust my arm forward, gulping for air as the limb followed my order.

This isn't my arm!

I scrambled, pulling and pushing at the bedsheets, frantically ripping at the hospital gown, pulling it up my legs to stare unbelievingly at the pale limbs which trembled with my shock.

Pale? I'm never pale!

"Oh my Gods," I whispered, gaze locked on the pale skin gracing my skin. "Oh, my Gods."

Voices were calling my name, the sound a

background to my panic attack. Hands touched me, but I didn't have the ability to register them.

This isn't my body.

My body was tanned and strong with zero tattoos and long elegant fingers that knew how to play the violin with dexterity and talent.

I flexed my fingers again, feeling the stiffness in their movement.

What the fuck happened?

One voice cut in. Deep, abrupt, unfamiliar.

"Emily!"

My gaze shot up, resting on Doctor Jenkins.

"What happened?" I croaked, my voice broken. "This isn't my body. This isn't *my* body."

"You have amnesia."

CHAPTER 2

Calvin

Apart from breaking my arm when I was eleven—I'd never had a need to be *in* a hospital. My grandparents were alive and of robust health, my parents the same. Even my siblings had rarely required a visit to this blocky, cold building, and when they had, I'd been left at home, sheltered from the reality of illness and the shroud of death that had settled into its very foundations.

I never even knew doctors had offices like this. Or at least not in a hospital.

I'd never had to think about a doctor's office before today.

I blew out a breath, my fingers pressed into my eyelids as I massaged them, trying to rub away the gritty weariness. My eyes were dry, and the last time I'd looked in a mirror, bloodshot. I knew my body required rest, but I couldn't seem to stop my mind from racing for longer than a few stolen minutes.

I dropped my hand, finally looking at the kindly man across from me. "What you're telling me is my wife doesn't remember anything?"

"That's not strictly correct." Doctor Jenkins knit his hands together on the desk, considering me with warm sympathy. "Retrograde amnesia is a tricky diagnosis. Emily retains familiar information, learned skills, and a substantial amount of her memories. Considering the significant trauma experienced during her accident, I'd considered this a miracle."

"What does she remember?"

"Everything up to New Year's Eve twenty-fourteen."

I blew out a long breath as the reality of her injury hit me. Emily didn't remember our wedding. Our laughter. Our holidays or dinners. Her sister's separation or recent reunion with her husband.

She doesn't remember the disintegration of our marriage.

I felt... bereft. Torn. The woman I knew wasn't the woman staring at me with a bemused expression from the middle of a hospital bed, her fingers tracing the beard on my face as if it were a foreign object.

Five years just... gone.

I found myself twisting my wedding ring around my finger over and over. The familiar weight somehow grounded me.

"What does this mean?" I finally asked.

"We can't know. It could be that her memories will return in time. Or it could be that this is Emily's new reality. You need to be prepared, Calvin, that she may never recover all or even any of the last five years."

I ran my fingers through my hair, tilting my head back to study the ceiling.

The doctor didn't speak, simply let me process.

"I honestly don't know what to do." I finally admitted, dropping my head to look back at him. "Our vows were in sickness and in health but...."

Dr. Jenkins gave me a small nod. "You were separated. On the brink of divorce, as I understand it." He shook his head. "No one would blame you for continuing with the divorce. Who you are is different to who Emily thinks you are. You're entitled to a life outside of her and this event. "

I'd blame myself.

I hadn't wanted the divorce to begin with. I fucking loved my wife. That had never been the problem. Love, sex, passion – we'd had all of it until we hadn't. Until....

"When can she come home?"

Dr. Jenkins cleared his throat. "It's been a week. All of Emily's vitals have stabilised, and she's regained all motor functions. Apart from her memories, Mrs. Jameson is in perfect health."

He unlocked his fingers, pushing some paperwork across the desk.

"These are Emily's release documents. I'm certifying that she is fine to return home. I'll want to see her as an outpatient for at least a few months while her brain injury continues to settle. Neurological injuries are notoriously unpredictable. Her concussion may continue to plague her for some time. Watch and track her headaches, mood swings, any irritability or personality changes. She could experience some light or noise sensitivity, smell or taste distortion, or even sleep disturbances. She may have trouble concentrating or issues with her short-term memory—though that doesn't yet seem to be the case. Note anything that appears out of the ordinary. Our tests thus far haven't shown anything beyond the occasional headache since she's stabilised, but in a familiar environment, the symptoms may present more readily."

Dr. Jenkins tipped his head slightly to the left, considering me with kind eyes. "I'd also recommend you both see a counsellor. Five years of lost memories will bring about grief, confusion, and anger. For both Emily and yourself." He tapped a card stapled to the top of the documents. "I've included the contact details of a clinic I'd recommend. They're local and very good at this type of counselling. They work with both partners and any interested family members."

I gathered the papers. "Thank you, Sir. I appreciate everything you and your team have done for my wife and me."

"Cal, you also need to watch her. I know we discussed what you found, and her condition supports our theory."

I swallowed, tasting bitter regret. "I understand."

He stood, holding out his hand. "Remember, take it slow, one day at a time. Don't overdo it—either of you. Watch for symptoms, try and get back into a routine, and contact me immediately if you see anything atypical."

Everything about this situation is atypical.

He gave my hand a firm shake, then

dropped it to walk around the desk to see me out. "Good luck, Calvin. I'll notify my team that they can start processing Emily's discharge."

"Thank you, Sir. And thank you and your team again for everything."

I walked out of his office, through the waiting room, and down the corridor heading toward Emily's room. I stopped two doors down, leaning heavily against the wall as the reality of our situation hit me like a Mack truck.

"Fuck," I muttered, looking down at the papers in my hands, pretending to read them as a distraction while I processed my thoughts.

I hadn't told Emily about our separation. Hadn't told her about the fact she wasn't the same woman I'd married five years ago. Years ago, I'd married a generous, kind, klutzy boho violinist who believed in following your dreams and loved dancing in the rain.

We'd met in college at a party. She'd been dressed in shorts that bared her gorgeous tanned legs; I'd been wearing a faded graphic shirt with a reference to The Office. We'd bonded over our shared love of sitcoms. I'd taken her back to my dorm, and we'd made love under the covers on the nasty single bed, her falling asleep on my chest and smothering me with her cascade of curls. I'd found a share-house to move into the following month

—complete with my own room and a queen bed.

For four years, we'd lived in various share-houses, travelling the world on dime budgets and eating some of the cheapest, tastiest food I'd ever eaten in my life. Both of us were trust fund babies from rich backgrounds—our parents more than willing to grant us the privileges that came with that upbringing. But Emily and I hated the noose that came attached to those privileges. We'd talked for innumerable nights about our desire to be our own people, to make our own way in the world.

And to achieve that, we'd lived on tight budgets, working multiple jobs to make ends meet.

I'd loved it. I'd loved the cold nights and the hot summers. The tiredness and the ache. I'd even loved the shitty ramen and cheap grilled sandwiches with soup. All because she'd been with me. Emily. My boho, clumsy, free-loving hippy who played the violin naked, who danced like no one was watching, who seduced me with laughter and smiles that lit her eyes in a way that I knew each one was from her soul.

And then, following our wedding, she'd gone. Not overnight. It wasn't as if a switch had been flicked following the wedding. No, this had been a slow transition. An almost imperceptible adjustment over a long period until one day, I came home and found a stranger where my wife had once lived.

Following a nasty altercation over Thanksgiving dinner, I'd decided to move out. The Emily I'd fallen in love with, the Emily I knew and loved, had been trapped behind a woman obsessed with looks and status. A woman with a better relationship with my mother—the devil—than me.

She doesn't remember any of it.

And thus, the crux of my current dilemma. My wife in the hospital room was not the wife I'd walked out on nearly two months ago. The wife in the hospital room was funny, kind and profuse with her praise and gratitude. She'd been devastated at the loss of her memories and yet took it all with a smile. She'd joked about my hair and compulsively and sincerely thanked every single nurse and doctor who assisted her, worrying about what the right present would be to get them as thanks.

She was the Emily I used to know. And I couldn't help but be glad, thankful, even hopeful about her return.

You're a fucking piece of shit.

I was a fucking jackass. An absolute piece of shit. I knew it because, honestly, who the fuck was glad their wife had lost her memories?

Apparently, this asshole. Fuck.

I had two options. Either tell her the truth and see where that took us, or start again—this time with the Emily I'd fallen in love with.

Don't be a douche. She deserves to know how fucked up we are.

I blew out a breath, folding the papers in my hands and tucking them into the back of my jeans.

I'll tell her tonight. Sit her down, and let her know what's up. Maybe when we see the counsellor, we can talk about how we got here... and what we can do to prevent it from happening again.

The hardest part would be erasing the hurt she didn't even know she'd caused. I knew I'd hurt her as well, but she didn't remember any of those moments. She'd reverted to our original relationship while I had years of memories to combat.

I'd only watched *Avengers Endgame* once. I'm sure the writers had meant it to be a movie about triumphing over adversity and overcoming great evil to save those who had been lost. But all I'd ever been able to concentrate on were the people who were left alive. Those who hadn't turned to dust. Those survivors had lived for years with their grief. They'd had to rebuild their lives and form new bonds and friendships. They'd lived through the slow decay of cities, through the recovery and clean-up.

Those were the ones I pitied. Not the ones who had gone and then returned. I'd always felt shitty for the survivors who'd rebuilt their lives only to be reverted back once more.

What about moving on? What about those who grieved and then got on with their life, trying to build a new future, new relationships, new memories in that post-life? And then, just as they'd begun to achieve some kind of normalcy, their loved ones had returned, and that process needed to begin again.

Fuck you're a morose bastard.

But I couldn't deny that's how I felt right now—like those people in the movie. The Emily I'd known, the Emily I'd grieved, had suddenly returned from the dead—leaving me shellshocked and impossibly conflicted.

Jesus fucking Christ, Cal. Pull your shit together.

I tried to shake off the shitty feeling. Tried to brush off the complex concoction of emotional baggage that currently sat on my shoulders as I headed to her room, reminding myself of Dr. Jenkins' advice.

Just take it slow, one day at a time.

CHAPTER 3

Emily

It was official. I'd been snatched from my life and placed in some kind of alternate universe.

As a believer in multi-dimensions, this was the only possible explanation for my current predicament—the actual reality that perhaps I was living with retrograde amnesia was too painful to contemplate. Hence, my current fixation on the parallel universe theory.

It's either that or you've somehow lost who you are.

And that thought was even more painful and absurd than the possibility of inter-dimensional travel.

My fancy phone beeped, a message coming in.

MOTHER-IN-LAW

I hear you've been discharged. I'll expect to see you for lunch at the club this week.

Of all the people I'd expected to be blowing up my phone, she wasn't one of them.

Cal drove us from the city down the coastal road toward Capricorn Cove. The city wasn't far, only an hour or so on a bad traffic day. We'd moved to the Cove the year before our engagement, the year after we'd graduated from college. I'd landed a job as a school music teacher at the local school while Cal had been forced into the family business, making the daily commute to the city for work.

If I'd ever doubted the diagnoses before, this drive cemented it—I had amnesia. The landscape looked at once familiar and foreign. New roads and houses had sprung up as if overnight, while unfamiliar businesses now resided in established store fronts making me question what was reality and what was fiction. Even natural objects had changed, familiar landmarks shaped by time and nature.

These incremental variations, some large, some small, were enough to unsettle me.

"How you doing over there?" Cal asked, hitting the indicator to take us up the cliff road.

"I mean...." I raised one shoulder in a half-shrug. "This feels a little surreal."

He chuckled. "I can imagine. I can't even think of what to point out to you. What to warn you about. I'm so familiar with everything that it's hard to remember what has changed."

I blew out a breath. "I'm sorry."

He shot me a look. "Don't be."

I bit my lip, watching the road. "Cal?"

"Mm?"

"This new house we have. Is it...."

How do I say this without sounding like a dick?

"What, baby?"

"Is it like these?" I plucked at the clothing he'd brought me to wear.

He frowned, briefly glancing over before he turned back to focus on the road. "Sorry, babe. Not sure I understand the question."

Fancy. Expensive. Tight. Something your mother would own.

"Very different to our little cottage?"

He let out a dry, humourless chuckle. "Oh yeah."

My stomach twisted in nervous knots. "But we love it?"

He frowned, then turned the car up a road

known as Millionaire's Row. My upset stomach clenched, nausea hitting me.

Unless Cal had made junior partner in the few years since he'd started at his family's company, there was no way we'd be able to afford a house on this street without dipping into the family coffers.

And we promised never to do that.

"I mean, you seem to," he finally said, as if unsure of how to answer me. "It's... different from the cottage. Different even from the house my parents gave us for our wedding."

"Th—th—they—they gave us a house?" I stuttered.

He nodded. "I have pictures somewhere; I'll dig them out."

"And we accepted it?" I clarified.

"We didn't really have a choice."

There's always a choice.

A whisper of the memory of Cal's voice tickled the back of my neck. College, our final year. We'd been considering our options for graduate jobs. His family had expected him to return to the fold. Move to the Cove, work in the city, and build up the business.

"Do you have a choice?" I'd asked him one night.

"There's always a choice, babe." He'd given me a small half-smile, his fingers tracing lazy circles on the palm of my hand. "But if I don't take this, then

we're gonna be living in poverty until I can find a job that pays a decent wage."

I'd looked around our small studio apartment with its second-hand furniture and chipped dishes. Our dinner had consisted of cheap cheese grated over some questionable spaghetti and red sauce that I'd brought home from my waitressing job.

It wasn't great. It wasn't even good. But we'd purchased everything ourselves. Every dollar we used, we'd earned. And that felt phenomenal.

I'd looked back at Calvin, pride burning deep in my chest. "It's your decision. I'll support whatever option you choose. I love you, Cal. I don't need fancy things. I just need you. Nothing is going to change that."

Cal signalled to the left, pulling up to a giant gated drive.

"Is this it?" I asked, straightening in my seat. The gates were ornate steel, swirling and ostentatious. The property was walled in, keeping prying eyes out.

"Yeah," he answered, hitting the button to open the barrier.

The metal slid open slowly, and Cal drove down the long gravel drive, giving me my first glimpse of the house.

My heart sank.

Oh. My. God. What have we become?

CHAPTER 4

Calvin

I watched Emily gingerly step through the door of our house. Her eyes were wide, her mouth shaped in a perpetual O as she looked up and up and up at the grand ceiling of our entry from which hung an obstinate chandelier.

I hated that fucking chandelier.

"Well, this is...." She swallowed. "Pretty?"

It sounded more like a question than a statement.

You chose it, baby girl.

She wore the most casual clothing I could find in her closet—designer activewear leggings with a cashmere sweater that cost more than any sweater had a right to.

The bandage would remain on her head for another two days. The injury, her pale and still bruised skin, coupled with her near-constant wide-eyed observations, lent her a waifish, vulnerable air.

Not at all the woman I'd married.

"Have we lived here long?" she finally asked, running her fingers absently along the entry wall.

"Two years."

She started at my words, her head twisting to give me that wide-eyed look once more "But..." she trailed off, biting her lip.

"But?" I promoted.

"It's so... sterile." She frowned, continuing into the house, glancing into rooms as we walked. "Where's the colour?"

"You paid an interior decorator a shit-ton of money to design this theme," I reminded her.

"What theme? White on white?" she asked as we reached the curved grand staircase.

"Actually, it's multiple shades of white – as you took great pains to tell me."

She blew out a breath, stepping aside so I could lead her up the stair.

"Where are our photos? Our pictures? Paintings?"

I felt that bittersweet pull of regretful hope. A feeling I'd fast become acquainted with.

Our starter house had been an old cottage on the edge of town. Mouldy and borderline decrepit, the cottage had been freezing in winter and a fucking sweatbox in summer. But we'd loved it.

Em had spent hours painting murals on every wall, sewing colourful curtains to hang across our windows, and building quirky things to display. Photos of every event imaginable had lined our walls, blending seamlessly into the murals. Pictures taken at family events, during travel, or at the dinner table on a Thursday night. Each perfect because they'd captured joyful memories.

During our first year in the cottage, I'd cracked, deciding it wasn't good enough and willing to dip into my trust fund to find us a better situation. Emily had refused to move, arguing that she liked the cold because it meant we needed to snuggle. That she loved the heat because it forced us outside and into the beautiful nights. It had been our first real fight, but we'd stayed.

The time we'd spent in that house were some of my favourite memories. We'd climb onto the roof, lying on a blanket she'd brought with her to watch the sun sink over the horizon as it painted the sea and sky multiple shades of pink, orange, and purple. All the while, I'd be praying the roof would hold our weight while living for those nights.

Emily had been colour and life, whimsy and grace, light and laughter, my beautiful wife. She'd been my definition of love.

Right up until my parents had moved us onto the Estate following our wedding. Then my lover of colour and joy had faded to a woman as brittle, sterile and cold as this house.

And I was the dirtbag who'd let it happen.

"The photos might be in the attic," I finally told her. "I can see if I can dig them out."

"But—" she stopped herself again.

The selfish part of me was glad she'd begun self-censoring. I had no answers for her questions. No reason or moment in time that I could point to which said *this*. This is when we lost our way. This is when it changed.

And I'm so fucking sorry it did.

"Our room is last on the right."

She followed me as I manoeuvred her bags through the door. I heard her sharp intake of breath and knew exactly when she realised that this was a different reality to the one we'd once lived.

The designer had described it as ruthlessly modern. I'd described it as a showroom. Our bedroom had zero personality. Clean lines, white tiled floors, white furniture, and bedding.

The only colour came from strategically placed items that held no memories or personal value. They'd been selected for their appearance from designer boutiques in the city, not for the joy of the memories they'd invoke.

"Where's our stuff?"

I dropped the bags, turning to find Em staring in bewilderment at the room, her colour high, her body shaking.

Fuck.

Distressed was too simple a word for the emotional breakdown she was experiencing.

"What stuff, baby?" I asked, approaching her like I would a frightened animal.

She pulled back, her arms making agitated gestures toward the room at large. "Our things! The photos. The bowls we bought in Cambodia. Photos of our engagement. That god-awful meerkat statue you gave me for our anniversary." She turned to me, tears glistening on her lashes. "Where's our meerkat statue, Calvin? Where is he?"

God, the statue. I hadn't thought of it in... too long.

"I'm not sure, baby. You wanted to give him to Goodwill when we moved from the—"

"No." She shook her head brutally, immediately clutching at it as if in pain. "No, no, no! I wouldn't have done that! I wouldn't have just given away our things as if they had no value. This...." She looked around, still clutching her head. "This isn't my house. This isn't my life."

She blinked up at me, one hand dropping to press against her lips. "Shit. Shit, shit, shit!"

"Emily—"

She whirled, racing for the door.

"Fuck!" I raced after her, catching her before she managed to get to the stairs.

"Let me go!" She screamed, kicking at my shins and attempting to beat at my chest. "Let me go! You're not my husband! This isn't my life!"

"Jesus, baby. Stop." I tried to soothe her, tried to pull her closer and wrap her in my arms. She broke, her body wracked with grief and confusion and sobs so hard I worried she'd vomit.

I let her clutch me close and let her cry until I was sure she wouldn't run. Then I bent slightly, boosted her legs up and settled them around my waist, carrying her to the bedroom. I sat on the edge of the bed, keeping her wrapped around me like a koala. Her face pressed to my chest, her sobs uncontrollable.

The selfish fucker in me trotted back out.

She's back. This time? Don't let her escape.

I shoved the thought away, burying the guilt deep.

It took a long time. Longer than even I had thought for Em to calm. By that time, I'd moved us onto the bed. We were lying side-by-side, front-to-front, my fingers running through her hair, her gaze locked on my chest as she let out the occasional sniffle.

She finally looked up at me, her eyes and nose red and swollen. "Can you tell me what happened? How we got here?"

I blew out a breath, my fingers stilling in her hair. "It's hard to know, really."

"Cal, I look in the mirror and don't recognise myself." She lifted a hand to finger to her chemically straightened hair. "My hair is different, my body is different, my clothes, our house." She dropped her hand to my chest. "Only you're familiar. Only you feel like home."

I closed my eyes, savouring her words.

"And yet you're different too. You don't.... Just tell me."

Where to start?

"To be honest, I don't really know. We got married. A bigger wedding than either of us wanted." I smiled, remembering our joy. "But we did what we said we would."

"Snuck away to town hall?"

I nodded. "The day before. You got married

in a dress you made. I was wearing the navy suit you liked. Our witnesses were a guy there to pay a parking fine and a woman who was seeking a divorce."

She chuckled. "I hope the divorcee didn't try to talk me out of it."

"Nah, she was still a believer in true love," I remembered watching my beautiful Em, her curves accentuated by the lace of the dress, walk down the aisle toward me. I remembered the smile that I couldn't contain, the laughter as we awkwardly pushed the rings onto each other's fingers. The taste of her kiss as she became my wife.

"I'm glad you have that memory," she said, sounding bittersweet. "I'm glad we did that."

"We have pictures," I told her, frowning as I tried to remember where our secret folder was. "We had our own private reception in the honeymoon suite at that BnB you loved."

"Madison's by the Sea?"

"Mm," I murmured, my fingers beginning to trail softly over her arm. "We ate burgers while sipping champagne directly from the bottle. Then made love on the giant bed while the sun went down."

She sighed, closing her eyes. "I wish I could remember."

I do too.

She blinked her glorious amber eyes open. "We were happy?"

"Blissfully so."

"Then what changed?"

I sighed, my fingers continuing to trail up and down her arm as I tried to dissect the last five years. "To be honest, I don't really know. It was incremental at first. We'd planned to go backpacking in Peru for our honeymoon. I had to work, but we were going to go in September, after the busy period. You said you wanted to get fit, so you started working out."

"Obviously, I liked it," she said with a wry smile gesturing to her body.

"That's the thing. I don't think you did." I dropped my hand, letting it settle on the bones of her hip. "It was like you were... trapped in a cycle. You became obsessed with status. You took advice from my *mother*."

Her nose wrinkled.

"Exactly." My mother was the last woman on earth you'd take any advice from. "Then you started to wear designer clothes. You told me it was because you hated when mum made comments about you when she saw you on the Estate."

"Wait. We lived on the Estate?" She sat up. "We agreed never to—"

"I know." I sat beside her, dragging a hand

through my hair. "They built a house on the parcel of land they purchased from the Morgans."

She groaned, placing a hand over her eyes. "Worst idea ever."

20-20 hindsight, babe.

"Yeah," I swallowed, knowing the worst was yet to come. "You quit your job after we moved in here. Said you didn't have time for it."

She blinked, her eyes widening. "Excuse me?"

I shrugged. "You started doing brunches and charity things in the city with mum."

"And you let me quit?"

"I figured if it made you happy...." I trailed off, knowing that was the chickenshit answer. "To be honest, by that stage, it was just easier to let you do you."

She frowned, "I don't understand."

"You weren't you anymore, Em." I struggled to put into words the changes that had occurred. "You'd told me to take the promotions dad kept offering at work even though I had in no way earned them. You told me to use the trust funds. You wanted this house, and you wanted personal training with a guy who cost a fuck more than I'd ever earned in a year before opening the family coffers. You wanted to vacation in places recommended by people who aren't anything more than fair-weather snobs who gossiped behind our backs."

I gestured at her body. "You started doing juice cleanses and something that involved wrapping yourself in plastic wrap. You'd buy expensive clothing and wear them once. You called Honey fat."

"Your sister? No!" Her hands covered her mouth, her expression horrified. "Oh my God, Cal. Oh my God. How... how did... who... who am I?"

A woman I loathed to love.

I pulled her in, her slight body wiggling into me as she struggled against more tears. "You're still you, Em. Under all the bullshit that happened, you're still a generous and loving person. We just have to... work to not let us go back to that."

She tilted her head up, her face beseeching. "But *why* did I become that? And if I became this woman, who did you become?"

A fucking great question.

"I can't answer the first. As to the second...." I paused, considering. This hadn't been one-sided. While Em had changed, I had too.

"I became a workaholic," I admitted. "You know, I actually can't think of the last time I turned my phone off or didn't work on the weekend."

Or came home before midnight. Or had an actual, uncontactable under any circumstance vacation.

I swallowed. "I abandoned you. I neglected our relationship and used money to try and solve our issues when what we really needed was time together."

Em watched me with solemn eyes, her face still puffy. "Are you happy, Calvin?"

"No," I wretched the word from my soul. "I haven't been happy since...."

Since when, Calvin?

I didn't have an answer. We sat in silence for a long time. Through the numerous windows, the sun began to drop in the sky, darkness coming early at this time of year.

"Did we go to Peru?" Em finally asked.

"You know, we never did get there."

Her hand found mine in the growing darkness, holding tight.

"Would... would you maybe like to go with me?"

I looked down at the woman beside me. She wore hope on her face.

"Yeah," I murmured, letting myself believe in this reality. Letting myself choose to see this accident as the wake-up call we both needed. "I'd love to take you."

Her lips lifted in a smile. "Okay."

"Okay."

CHAPTER 5

Emily

I'd been home for two weeks, and it had become painfully obvious that the intimacy Cal and I had once shared had eroded over time. Every time I reached for him, pressed a kiss to his cheek, wrapped an arm around his waist, or reached out to hold his hand, every single time he looked surprised.

He never pushed me away, instead lingering a little longer as if he wanted more of this easy affection. As if he had been starved for even one little touch.

We hadn't had sex yet. I didn't quite know how. I mean, I knew *how*, just not how to approach this.

I exited the shower, pausing to look at my

dripping body in the full-length mirrors lining the wall of the room. They were anti-fog, meaning you got an uninterrupted view of every crack and crevice of your body from disrobing to dressing.

Which confused me. Who wanted to see that every day?

I scrutinised my body, examining myself with a kind of fascinated curiosity.

This person in the mirror didn't look familiar. My skin was pale, indicating a preference for the indoors, which was strange as I had never been that kind of person. There were new marks and bumps, wrinkles and folds. And the tattoo. A simple but beautifully ornate comet.

I shook my head at the mirror, turning away. I was all for being healthy, but this didn't feel like I'd attempted to achieve a healthy medium.

I covered my unfamiliar body in designer clothing that I hated and walked downstairs to my makeshift music room, having found that the only room in this monstrous house with any kind of acoustics was the library.

I felt strangely lonely as well as nervous and unsettled. Calvin had returned to work today, promising to be home in time for dinner, but that was hours away, and I found I had little to distract me from my thoughts.

I could have called Collins to come spend today with me, but I didn't want to disturb her simply because I felt uncomfortable in my own home. Collins had been at the hospital each day, Nick close on her heels.

It hadn't escaped my notice that the photos she'd shown me during these visits had evidenced my growing brittleness as the years progressed. My openness hidden behind pursed smiles, fake laughter, and social media-worthy poses.

It also hadn't escaped my notice that Collins and Nick were my only visitors. Not even my parents or Cal's siblings had made the effort to visit.

What did you do?

I pushed away the unsettling thoughts and picked up the violin, placing it just so on my shoulder. I'd discovered my violin on the top shelf of my closet under an inch of dust.

Yet another pleasure you gave up for some reason.

My fingers moved as I began my warm-up, the joints stiff and the notes stunted. Another reminder of a pleasure that had been brushed aside.

I practised for two hours, losing myself in the movement and sound, trying to recapture the magic that had once flowed so easily from my hands. At the end of the session, I felt simultaneously elated and overwhelmed. The piece was simple, but I'd stuttered through it, the notes coming a beat too slowly, the sound a fraction too pitched. It would be more days of this, likely taking hundreds of hours to reclaim the practised ease with which I used to play – the thought of which was daunting. And yet, I was proud of the effort, proud of my body and my mind for trying.

I dropped the bow on the stand and replaced the violin, taking a moment to stretch my protesting muscles.

The library, despite being the best room in the house acoustically, creeped me the fuck out. When Cal had first given me a tour and mentioned we had a library, I'd been thrilled, expecting thick carpets or perhaps rugs over warm wooden floors. I'd envisioned a heavy stone fireplace with comfortable seating or perhaps a light, airy room with window seats.

The room had defied and devastated all expectations. Floor-to-ceiling bookcases filled with display books and knick-knacks that had been chosen not for reading enjoyment but for display. In fact, one whole shelving wall had every single book turned spine side in, the pages the only viewable part. Another was filled with books covered in white paper – a theme, I was told, that had been championed by celebrities. The final wall held a mishmash of encyclopaedias and law texts.

I loitered by the white wall fighting a tide of frustrated anger as I stared at the idiocy of the covered books. Without thinking, almost as if my hand was detached from my body, I reached for a book and ripped it from the shelf. In a violent action, I used my other hand to rip the stupid white jacket free, revealing a deep red cover of Neil Gaiman's American Gods.

The anger overpowered me, and I reached for another book, pulling it free and ripping the white off to reveal a beautiful peacock blue. I replaced it, reaching for the next and the next, ripping and replacing in a systematic, almost compulsive rhythm.

As I reached the end of the first shelf, a trail of white paper following in my wake, I pulled a book free, knocking it against a heavy metal art piece and sending it crashing to the floor. It hit one of the whitewashed wood floorboards with a crack, sending it bouncing up on one end and sliding out of place. I blinked for a moment, staring at the carnage before letting out a heavy sigh and dropping to my knees.

"Fuck," I muttered, reaching for the broken floorboard and pulling it away from the hole.

"Great job, Emily. How you gonna explain this mess?"

It was only after I'd pulled it free and set it to the side that I realised I hadn't broken anything. Under the loose board, nestled in a void between the concrete slab, sat two items. One was a long airtight container, the other a large fireproof safe, the dial facing up toward me.

I reached first for the safe. Heaving and panting, I pulled it up by the case handle, ignoring the scraping sound as it dragged over the edge. I crouch before it, wracking my brain for a possible combination.

My birthday, Cal's birthday and our anniversary didn't work. I paused for a moment, then twisted a final combination, letting out a delighted squeal when it clicked open.

"God damn it, Cal. Our sex date? Really?" I muttered, pushing the lid back with a small smile. Our sex date had happened three weeks after our first official night together. I'd surprised him with handcuffs and lingerie, he'd surprised me with three orgasms in half an hour.

The contents were fairly benign. Marriage and birth certificates, a USB labelled 'photos', passports which were sadly bereft of adventures.

I replaced the documents, shut the safe then reached into the void, pulling the storage box free. Inside was an unexpected treasure trove.

"Diaries," I whispered, pulling the precious journals free. I opened one, catching on the date neatly printed at the top of the page.

19 July 2017

I sifted through the journals, finding them to be a patchwork of the years I'd lost. I found the earliest, starting January 1 2015, and immediately commenced reading, trying to digest the words on the page and translate them into memories locked deep inside me.

Today Cal woke me with kisses on my toes.

The entries were sporadic, some weeks apart, some hours after one another. I'd written of our engagement, of the pressure in the lead-up to the wedding. I'd documented in glorious detail our wedding day – our *real* wedding day, at town hall followed by the night at the cheap seaside BnB. Tears filled with regret and rueful longing flowed down my cheek as I turned each page.

> *I miss our wedding day. Our REAL wedding day. Today was awful. Mum and Dad fought in the car on the way to the church. Collins had to run interference while trying desperately to catch Nick's attention. Nick spent most of it on the phone – I'm worried he's going to break her heart.*

I brushed away tears, knowing that I'd predicted correctly. Collins had told me about their separation and only recent reconciliation. I hurt and rejoiced for my sister but mostly felt strangely disconnected from all that had happened. And that in itself was distressing.

> *I know I shouldn't write this, shouldn't give it head space or waste the words on the page. But I can't shake the words, and I need to get*

it out. I overheard Cal's cousins in the bathroom. They were complaining that I was an embarrassment to him. That I was uncouth and naïve and was only acceptable due to my parent's fortune. Someone joined them, then another, and before I knew it, I was trapped in a toilet cubicle listening to a flock of women pull everything about me apart.

I raised a hand to my mouth, absently biting on my fist as I turned the pages, picking up journal after journal and reading my descent into self-hate.

We went out for dinner with Cal's parents. His mother commented that I looked pregnant.

Cal surprised me with flowers and breakfast in bed. I love this beautiful man.

Cal's mother hired me a personal

*trainer. She said I need to lose
weight. I don't think I do, but I
don't want to embarrass him. I
want Cal to be proud of me.*

*I went to Cal's work dinner
tonight. I need to buy more designer
clothes. I hate embarrassing him,
but I didn't know they'd all be so
fancy.*

I opened the last diary hours later, a sickness burned into my soul. The words on the page were written by a person I didn't recognise. A woman so desperate for approval that she'd begun to hate herself, hate her body, her thoughts, her life.

She said horrible things and wrote in these diaries seeking forgiveness but was unable to stop. She pushed away her husband but wanted him with such a burning passion that it ached. She was in purgatory, waiting for the inevitable moment her husband left her.

My tears had long since ceased, burned away by shame.

I opened the soft leather cover of the final

diary to the first page.

> *Thanksgiving. Cal left me today. He said he'd be back for his things in a few days.*
>
> *I can't breathe. I said unforgivable things to Honey. Cal's sister didn't deserve my censure.*
>
> *It's just... when I look at her, I see her gorgeous confidence. Her full body. Her beauty and wit, and I know I can't measure up. I know I'm stuck battling this rotting, embarrassing, horrible shell I live in.*
>
> *I'm lashing out. I'm hurting. And I want everyone to hurt as much as I do.*
>
> *Gods, why am I so awful? Why can't I stop?*

I let out a shuddering breath, unable to believe the words before me. He'd left. He'd walked out. I read on.

Cal agreed to meet me for lunch.
We went to a diner near his work.
It hurt to see him watching me with
such angry and disappointed,
hopeless eyes.

It's Christmas. Cal spent it with
Honey and her new partner. I think
Willodean went as well. Collins is in
London.

I'm all alone.

And I have no one to blame but
myself.

I just want things to go back to
before everything got so messed up.

I wish I could go back.

I need to change. I have to.

I sucked in a breath, realising the next page
contained the last entry—it was dated the day
of my accident.

It's New Year's Eve. I invited
Cal over, but he refused. Said it

was better if we waited to see each other at the counselling session. But the marriage counsellor can't get us in until late January.

I can't live without him. It hurts. Everything hurts.

He wants a divorce, and all I want is him.

Gods, how did I let this happen? How did we end up here?

I ache for my husband. My heart feels as if it is breaking, shattering. Everything hurts.

I have to change. I can't let him leave. I can't. He's the only man I've ever loved. He's the only man I will ever love.

And he deserves better. We both do.

I reread the words, unable to bear the aching in my chest.

"Emily?" Cal's voice came from the hall. "You home?"

I choked out a strangled sound, unsure if I should allow him to find me like this.

"Em?" he called again, sounding worried. "Pretty Eyes?"

"Library," I finally answered, my voice breaking.

His reassuring footsteps preceded him. His heavy tread beautifully familiar. The world may be different, his face may be slightly older, and his hair now starting to show grey. My body may be unfamiliar, our house completely unlike our former home. But Cal's footsteps, his even, solid, heavy gait made me feel warm and reassured. Comforted that my man was here.

"Oh, Pretty Eyes." He stood at the door surveying the damage. The remains of the white paper I'd torn from the books littered the floor. Piles of diaries sat on either side.

"Emily." He walked to me, crouching down, not touching me just yet. "What happened?"

I swallowed, desperate to bring moisture to my mouth. Desperate to admit the truth.

"I discovered who I am now," I whispered, unable to look him in the eye. "And I hate her."

CHAPTER 6

Calvin

I pulled a weeping Emily into my arms.

She found the diaries.

I hated this. Hated she'd discovered the items I'd locked away.

I'd found the hateful things the day after her accident. I'd returned to our house for the first time in months to pack her a bag. In our bedroom, I'd found the diaries spilled out across our bed.

Reading the despair on each page, I'd been struck by how our miscommunication had escalated to this point.

I'd hidden them, wanting to shield this from her. To keep her protected from what had been our reality for as long as possible.

Fear stabbed my gut, my body turning to ice. *Would she change again?*

"That's it," I whispered, rocking her gently as she sobbed. "I've got you, baby. You just let all that out. Let go of it all. There's no need to hate yourself because I love you. Collins loves you. Nick loves you. We all love you."

She cried harder at my words, her voice broken and muffled as she said something against my chest.

"What?" I asked, still rocking her. "I can't hear you, Pretty Eyes."

She tilted her head back, watching me with a sad, broken gaze. "How can you love me? I'm a monster."

I pulled her back in, allowing her to cry as I tried to process, trying to capture the right words to reassure her.

As she settled, her cries lessening, I seized my chance.

"I hid your diaries after the accident. I hid them after reading them. I hid them knowing they would fill the gaps in your memory, but also knowing the words weren't worth the paper they were written on."

I blew out a long breath, continuing to rock her, feeling her still, knowing she was listening. "If you're a monster, I'm the devil. Because I never fucking knew. Not until the accident. I never even questioned why you were doing things like fad diets and personal shopping. Just thought it was making you happy." I finally looked down at her. "I slept beside you for five years, Emily, and never once knew you hated our life. Never even fucking suspected it. It took a man in a coat after you passed out and crashed your car to tell me what was before my own eyes."

I shook my head. "You passed out, baby. Passed out on an icy patch of road and ran straight into a tree. How the fuck am I the kind of man you deserve when I never even saw how much you were hurting?"

She shuddered under my hands, pressing herself close. "I don't remember, Cal. I still can't remember any of it. This life, that time, all the things I said. I thought maybe I would. Maybe something would prompt it. But...."

"It's gone."

She nodded. "All of it. And I don't know if that's a blessing or a curse."

I didn't either. Because as much as I loved my wife, as much as I loved that I had the woman I'd fallen in love with back, I was fucking angry. Angry that she had no memory of our life together. Angry at myself for being a selfish dick who'd retreated into work rather than support my wife when she needed me.

Angry I'd allowed this to happen. Angry, I'd stepped away from being the man she'd fallen in love with.

Fuck, I was angry that I thought I even had a right to be angry.

Weak piece of shit.

"I... I think I need to do counselling," Emily whispered into the quiet. "And not just for the head injury. But for... for this." She gestured at the diaries. "And for us too."

I nodded.

"I don't remember hating our life or the slow decline of our relationship. But I need time to process and to appreciate and learn to love who I am now. I need time to come to terms with our reality and to work out who you are now, too."

I brushed hairs away from her cheek. "You always were the smarter one."

She smiled, but it faded quickly. "Can we come back from this? Can we find our way back?"

I didn't rush my answer. I didn't want to give her platitudes or make her feel that I didn't take her, us or our life together seriously.

"Yeah, I know we can." I pulled her closer. "Leaving you was the hardest fucking thing I ever did."

"But you left because I called your sister fat."

"I left because you did that and then didn't take ownership of the hurt it caused." That day was seared into my soul.

"I wish I could remember," Em whispered. "I want to apologise to Honey."

"If you want, I could invite them over for dinner." I offered, knowing it would cost Honey to come but hoping it might repair their relationship.

"I'd like that."

I nodded once, sealing the deal. She settled in my arms, quiet and pensive.

We stayed that way for a long time, sharing air and warmth. I couldn't recall the last time we'd done this, just been together.

"Cal?"

"Mm?"

"I hate this house."

I barked out a laugh, pulling back and groaning when I found that my ass had gone numb.

"I'm serious," Emily told me, her cheeky grin in place. "It's like some kind of white hells cape."

"It's not that bad," I chuckled.

"It is," she insisted. "It's a clinical iceberg of

nothing. I get a headache just looking at it each day."

"Are you sure the headache isn't from your injury?" I teased.

She rolled her eyes. "Too soon."

"You want to go to Home Depot?"

"What, now?"

I shrugged. "Why not. They're open late. We could get some paint. At least splash something on the walls of the bedroom to help you stop questioning your sanity."

Her smile was glorious. "Can we get some burgers on the way home?"

"Oh shit," I laughed. "You won't remember the Bronze Horseman."

"The what?" Em tilted her head to the side, her hair sliding off her shoulder.

"Baby, you're gonna love it."

CHAPTER 7

Calvin

"Really?" I asked, placing my hands on my hips as I surveyed the cart. "I said we could buy paint, Em, not the whole fucking store."

"It's just a few things," she protested.

I'd been gone for less than five minutes to get some paintbrushes, and in that time, she'd managed to add a rug, colourful bedding, picture frames, and a meerkat print shower curtain to the six pails of paint.

I held up the curtain. "Do we need this?"

"Yes. The mirrors in our bathroom freak me out."

I dropped it back in, knowing this was a battle I was about to lose. And that knowledge fucking delighted me. This whole evening, the car ride, the shopping, the fucking meerkat print shower curtain, all of it. I couldn't describe how fucking happy I was, and all over a trip to Home fucking Depot.

But it's more than a trip. It's the spark in Em's eyes, it's the smile on her lips, and it's the knowledge that you – you jackass- haven't fucked this up.

"You done?" I asked, enjoying her delight.

"Mm. Maybe." She glanced down an aisle, then shook her head. "We can come back, right?"

"Of course."

"Okay." She patted the side of the cart. "Then let's get this paid for. I'm hungry."

The woman at the checkout laughed as she swiped our purchases. "New house?"

"No," Emily replied happily. "Just redecorating."

The woman reached over, scanning the paint cans. "Hope you kids have a great time. Redecorating is fun, but good lordy, it can be messy."

Em hip-bumped me, shooting me a flirty smile. "I can handle dirty."

I slung an arm around her shoulder, pulling her in to nuzzle her neck, making her laugh. "Yeah, you can."

I paid and then led us out, navigating the

cart through the car park. We chatted as we loaded purchases, chatted as we got in the car, and laughed as I drove us through town to the main street that ran parallel to the marina.

"Wow," Em murmured, her head turned to look out her window. "This has changed."

"A family purchased the marina last year; they're looking to redo it. But Main Street has slowly been upgrading for a while."

I turned into a rare vacant street spot, easing to a stop. We climbed out, and I came around, swinging an arm around her shoulders and guiding her down the street.

"Do you remember Ella Bronze?" I asked, trying to figure out how long it had been.

Em shook her head.

"Well, Ella is a local business owner. She started up the Bronze Horseman a couple of years ago with her co-owner, Anika Sharif, who's the chef. It's pretty successful. Her fiancé only moved to town this past year, but he purchased the marina and is planning upgrades."

Em tipped her head back, raising an eyebrow. "Are you normally this interested in local businesses?"

I hesitated, wondering how much to reveal.

"Normally, no," I admitted, deciding to start

our new life off with honesty. "But in this case, yeah."

"In this case?"

"Let's find a table, then we can talk."

We entered the Bronze Horseman, and I heard Em suck in a breath.

"This is so cool," she murmured, looking around at the restaurant. It had a classy, speakeasy vibe that in no way detracted from the coastal setting outside. The fire in the giant hearth crackled away while an acoustic mix of classic rock filtered through the noise of the diners.

"Welcome to the Bronze Horseman, table for two tonight?" A waitress asked, picking up two menus.

"Yes please."

She led us through the busy space, making a beeline for a snug little booth toward the back of the room.

"Cal?"

We both stopped, twisting to look at my sister and her date at one of the tables close to the fire.

Honey's gaze darted from me to Em and back. I caught the subtle move of her boyfriend, Sheriff Tristan Rodriguez, as he narrowed his eyes on Em, his body stiffening.

"Honey?" Emily asked, stepping toward them.

"Hey," my sister replied, rising from her table to greet us. "Emily, I'm glad to see you're doing well. I was going to drop by, but...."

Em tensed, her body rigid under my arm.

"But you've been historically horrible to Honey, and I refused to allow her to subject herself to a toxic environment even for politeness," Tristan said, moving to Honey's side.

There was a beat of silence after his comment.

"Umm," Honey murmured, glancing up at Tristan. "I mean—"

"I'm sorry," Em burst out, her hands coming up to wring nervously in front of her. "I know I don't remember the situations or the words I said, but I'm really sorry for the hurt and pain I caused. You're gorgeous and talented, and you were always kind to me when Cal and I first started dating. I just...." She took a step forward, then faltered. "I just hope that if we can't be friends, then we can at least start over."

Both Honey and Tristan blinked at her impassioned words. They glanced at each other, a wealth of information passing between them, and I couldn't help – even if he pissed me off a little – being glad my sister had found herself a good guy.

"I'd like that," Honey finally said, turning back to Emily. She offered a small smile. "Did you two want to join us?"

"Another time," I replied, reaching over to draw Emily back to my side. "This is our first date since the accident. I don't think I want my sister and the town Sheriff playing chaperone."

My joke broke the tension, Emily leaned into me, her body loosening, while Tristan and Honey chuckled.

"Okay, brother of mine." Honey waved a hand at me. "Get out of *my* date."

I shifted away, wrapping her in a quick hug, aiming a chin jerk at Tristan before pulling back. "I'll call you to set up a time to catch up."

"Sounds great," she replied, offering Em a smile. "Have a good night."

"Thanks, you too," Em replied.

I slung an arm over her shoulder, and we followed the hovering waitress, no doubt gossip fodder for the rest of her night.

Em settled in the booth, and I sat across from her. The waitress handed us menus, took our drink orders and coats, recited the specials then disappeared. Under the table, I kicked off one shoe, finding her feet with mine. Em startled, her face lifting from the menu to laugh.

"Really? Footsies?"

I purposefully concentrated on the menu, pretending to be interested in the words. "No idea what you're talking about."

My toes wiggled, tickling her ankle, and she pulled back, giggling. "You're an idiot."

"Cal, Emily, hey! Long time no see, Team Jameson. How've you kids been?" Ella, the owner, sauntered up to our table, placing drinks on it with practised ease.

"Good," I answered for us, discarding the menu and offering her a grin. "How's wedding planning going?"

"Horrible," she said cheerfully. "Gunnar wants a big wedding. I want to elope. We're compromising by having a big wedding."

We chuckled.

"Which he, of course, isn't interested in planning." She shook her head, her long dark hair falling around her shoulders. "Add in that we're a few waiters short, and it's all hands on deck around here. Now, what can I get you?"

Emily had a slight crease between her eyebrows as she stared at Ella. "What would you recommend?"

"Oh, so many things," Ella laughed. "But if you're really interested, I can bring out the chef's sampler."

"Sounds good, Cal?"

I nodded. "We'll do that."

"Perfect! And FYI, Emily's side of the booth can't be seen from the floor." Ella scooped up the menus giving us a saucy smile and wink before disappearing.

Emily burst out laughing, the slight frown completely wiped away. "She's cool."

"Yeah."

"Are we friends?"

I swallowed, shaking my head even though I knew it would cause her pain. "No. You only go out with women from the club or wives of some of my work colleagues."

"The club?"

I cleared my throat. "The country club."

"Ah." She nodded thoughtfully. "And these wives, are we close?"

I shrugged, unable to answer.

"Hm." She reached for her glass, taking a sip of the soda. "No one has messaged me or reached out since my accident." She pulled her phone out of her pocket, sliding it across the table to me. "I had a look through my messages and emails. The calendar says the last time I went out with anyone was just after Thanksgiving. But I don't have even one text after that."

She swallowed, looking off to the side. "If I

had to guess, I think I told someone about our separation, and they all bailed on me."

"I'm sorry."

She shrugged, "I can't miss what I don't remember. But...." She trailed off.

"But?" I prompted when she didn't resume.

Em shook herself, breaking away from whatever thought had taken hold. "I guess this is just another sign of how much I've changed." She laughed, but it sounded bitter. "I'll add it to the list of things to improve."

I reached across the table, threading my fingers with hers.

"Hey," I said, waiting for her to look at me. Finally, her pretty eyes met mine. "I'm here. I'm not going anywhere. Shit happens, but we all change." I smiled. "You told me that."

"I did?"

"Yeah, on our wedding day." I stood, leaning over the table and pressing a kiss to her mouth. "We're not set and forget. We grow, we change, and we make mistakes. The important thing is that we choose to change. And we choose each other."

She nodded, tears glistening on her eyelashes. "When you left, did you regret it?"

"Every day. But I didn't know how to get through to you. Just like you didn't know how to get through to me."

There was quiet in our booth, the sounds of the restaurant swirling around us but outside of our cocoon.

"I choose you, Calvin. But the longer I stay in that house, in this life, the less I feel comfortable."

I blew out a breath. "I know."

She blinked at me. "You do?"

"Yeah," I admitted. "And I have a plan."

She leaned forward, her head tilting slightly to one side. "A plan?"

I nodded, about to explain when Ella reappeared with plate-laden arms.

"Here we are, love-bugs. Two chef's samplers." She set four plates down on the table. "We have a serving of burger sliders – pulled pork, lamb deluxe, and a cheesy halloumi which is to *die* for. On the middle plate, you have pan-fried squid and baby octopus, the bowl contains a grain salad to compliment, and it is freaking amazing if I say so myself. Lastly, we have a delicious plate of chicken wings – today's flavours are tandoori, honey soy, and classic barbecue." She disappeared, reappearing a moment later with two serving plates. "Here you go. You guys need any drink refills?"

"No, thank you, I think we're okay for now,"

Em replied, looking at the food. "This looks and smells amazing."

"Thanks, my chef is the freaking bomb." She clapped her hands together, "Just call if you need anything further, otherwise enjoy!"

In a swish of hair and smiles, Ella left.

"Wow," Em said, licking her lips. "Where do we even start?"

"Sliders," I decided, reaching for half of the lamb. "These look fucking good."

We split the slider, immediately groaning as we bit into it.

"Holy God," Em groaned, closing her eyes as she chewed. "This is heaven."

I couldn't argue. A pretty girl across from me, great food, and a sense of rightness that had been sadly missing from my life.

"So," Em said as she finished the slider and began spooning salad onto her plate. "Your plan?"

I swallowed, suddenly feeling sweaty. "We can talk about it later," I hedged.

She waved a hand at me dismissively. "No, wanna hear."

I watched her serve food onto my plate, reaching for my beer to try and wet my suddenly dry mouth. "So, the house you hate?"

"Mm?" Em hummed, a smile playing at the corners of her mouth.

"I want to sell it."

Em paused, fork held mid-raise. "Sell it?"

"Yeah," I blew out a breath. "And quit my job."

"Quit—okay." She lowered her cutlery. "Gonna need further information."

"I want to invest in the marina." I blew out a breath, a weight lifting. "I fucking hate my job. I hate the pressure, hate the people I work with, hate that I'm answerable to my dad, and that means every single person there hates me but still kisses my ass."

I ran a hand through my hair. "I want to be closer to home. I want to spend time with you and do something meaningful. Something I enjoy."

"And investing in the marina will give you that?" She asked.

"Yes and no. The marina is a start. I've done the figures. Our white horror of a home tripled in price in the last three years. I got an appraisal, and if we sell it, I'll have the capital to buy into Gunnar's development. I want to take the knowledge I developed working for dad and plug it into my own ventures. I honestly believe that with Gunnar's knowledge, my financial know-how, and Ella's hospitality experience, we'd be a good team to revamp Capricorn Cove."

"Cal, this sounds—"

I braced, resigning myself for rejection.

"—amazing!" Emily bounced on her seat. "Tell me more! How did this start? When do you want to sell? Why did we just buy paint for a house we're about to leave?"

I laughed, relaxing in my seat, her shoeless feet finding mine under the table.

"I thought we weren't playing footsies." I grinned.

She shrugged. "This announcement deserves a round of footsies."

"Only footsies?"

The mood in the booth shifted. Her body stilled, a flush colouring her cheeks. "What did you have in mind?"

I glanced out at the restaurant, but Ella was right. The angle of this booth meant that unless you were standing right at the end of it, you couldn't see shit.

"How far you wanna take this?" I asked, food forgotten.

Em licked her lips. "Guide me."

My dick leapt at her words, pressing hard against the zipper of my jeans.

Fuck.

Guide me was a game we'd played back in college. Stupid kids, in love and ready to explore the intimacies of our relationship, we'd devised this game where if she asked me to guide her, then I'd tell her what I wanted in the most explicit way possible.

"Baby," I murmured, my voice gruff. "I wanna see your pretty tits."

She shuddered, her breath no more than a pant as she slowly reached down. I waited, cock throbbing, aware of the people only inches away from us, as Emily slowly lifted her cashmere sweater and pulled it off, setting it beside her on the seat.

Dressed in nothing but a thin camisole, her nipples pressed against the fabric as her hands slowly drifted back down.

"Skin, Pretty Eyes. I wanna see the colour of your nipples. I wanna see them standing in the cool air."

She didn't hesitate. Her hands pulled the camisole up, and a moment later, her breasts were bared to my gaze.

I moaned, unable to keep myself away. I got out of the booth, quickly slipping around and coming to slide in beside her.

"Cal, what—?"

I cut her off with a brutal kiss. My hands covered her gorgeous tits, no longer as full as they used to be, but they were just as glorious and responsive as ever.

Em melted, her soft mews of pleasure lost in my mouth. I ran a thumb over her nipple, and she bucked under me, a familiar inadvertent request for more.

"Baby," I murmured against her lips. "You're delicious."

Em squirmed, her hand snaking down to cup me through my jeans.

"Please," she whispered against my mouth. "Please."

"Fuck." I pulled back, removing her hand and pinning it to her breast. "Keep that there."

She did as told, massaging the flesh, an offering to me in the most erotic of ways.

We were in the fucking public. My sister and her Sheriff boyfriend were mere feet away. And here I was with a half-naked Em, my hand diving down the front of her pants to stroke her clit and the biggest hard-on of my life.

"Quiet," I warned her, leaning in. "I'll let you come if you're completely silent."

She nodded, biting her lip, her eyes glazed with desire, her body completely pliant under my hands.

I shifted my fingers, finding her clit. Her eyes snapped shut, and only the barest of whimpers escaped her, barely perceptible even to me.

I grinned, ignoring the ache in my cock as I touched her. I pressed and swirled, drawing twitches and silent gasps from Emily. Her face flushed, her eyes screwed shut, and she pumped her hips into my hand until I hit the spot she was searching for. Her head tipped back, her body clenching as she came, glorious, beautiful and utterly silent.

"Good girl," I praised against her lips. "Come for me, Pretty Eyes. You deserve this."

She came down a moment later, falling against the back of the booth, her breasts rising and falling as she panted.

"Okay?" I asked, moving to pull down her camisole and readjust her pants.

"Perfect," she whispered, eyes still closed. "Just perfect."

Yeah, you are, baby.

"Come here," I pulled her up, tucking her into my side and pressing a kiss to her head. "Love you, Em."

"Love you too." She nudged my side, shaking a finger up at me. "But that doesn't mean I'm sharing the last slider."

"No, not even for that climax?"

"Not even if you sell the house and move us back to the cottage."

I raised an eyebrow. "You *want* to move back to the cottage?"

"Yeah." She shrugged, taking a large bite of her burger. "It was a happy home."

I spooned up a mouthful of the salad, chewing thoughtfully.

It was a happy home. Ain't that the truth.

CHAPTER 8

Emily

We arrived back at the house late, the moonlight glinting off the numerous windows.

"You know," Cal said as he pulled to a stop in the drive. "It's not a bad house."

It wasn't. It just wasn't home.

"True," I muttered, unbuckling. "But I just... it doesn't feel happy."

It was late, but he still emptied the car, piling the cans of paint and various items in the entry.

"Come on," he said, grunting as he lifted the rug. "Grab the bedding and your shower curtain."

"Wait, now?"

"Yeah," he called over his shoulder, heading for the stairs. "You're not gonna let me fuck you in a white bed or in the shower while that mirror is there." He paused halfway up the stairs, turning to look at me, the rug slung over one shoulder. "Wanna be inside you, baby, more than anything else in this fucking life."

With that, Cal turned, striding up the stairs and leaving me weak-kneed and wet at his words.

"Well," I cleared my throat and stooped to scoop up the packaged bedding and curtain. "I guess I'm getting luckier tonight."

In the bedroom, I found Cal rolling out the rug, placing it just so by the bed. I'd chosen a watercolour print, the vibrant blues, pinks, and purples faded into each other. The splash of colour was a welcome intrusion against the stark white.

Without thinking, I knelt on it, running my fingers through the thick weave.

"Fuck it," Cal said, dropping to his knees and reaching for me. "I can't wait."

I squeaked as he pulled me down, hovering over me. His hands ran over my body, pushing my sweater and camisole off and immediately going to my pants to pull them off.

In but a second, he had me naked and withering as he kissed his way down my body.

"Cal," I panted, his head dipping further to my abdomen. "Cal...."

"Need a taste."

His tongue dipped, and I jerked as his mouth tasted my wet need.

We both groaned, desperate and throbbing.

"More," he demanded, pushing my legs open and taking what I offered.

I fisted his hair, holding him to my core as he played me like an expert conductor, my body singing with need under his mouth.

"Cal—" I bit off my protest, body clenching and writhing as the orgasm broke, unexpected but welcome.

"Yes!" He surged up, giving me no space to recover. His cock bridged my entrance, and I welcomed him, arching up.

He paused for a moment, then slammed into me, forcing my body to accommodate him.

I loved it, I hated it, I wanted more, I wanted... I needed... I...

I lost all sense of self, giving in to him, letting him control my reactions and responses. Letting him lead.

"Fuck," he barked. "Gonna come. You feel too goddamned good."

His admission drove me over the edge, and I came again, losing myself as he roared his pleasure, bottoming out and emptying his cum into me.

We crashed to the floor, a wet patch soaking our new rug.

I tried to catch my breath while my body shuddered with aftershocks. I'd never come so quickly or consistently before. It was as if he had discovered a secret switch in the years between then and now.

And to be honest, maybe he had. And who was I to complain when five years of additional experience, Cal was a superb lover.

Eventually, the chill of the room set in, forcing us to redress. I cleaned up, finding him remaking the bed with the colourful sheet set we'd purchased.

"It could have waited 'til morning," I told him, leaning against the door jamb and enjoying the view.

"Told you, not gonna fuck you on anything that you hate."

I tsked. "You're really missing out on some serious hate sex, then."

He paused in his sheet-tucking efforts. "Angry sex?"

I shrugged, amused at his hopeful expression. "You'll never know now."

He looked so forlorn that I took pity on the poor man.

"Tell you what. Next week, swap out the sheets for the white ones for a day. I'll be a naughty girl then."

"You're always a naughty girl," he told me, walking around the bed to straighten the top sheet.

"Never."

"Always."

We grinned at each other, the argument familiar and comfortable.

When he was finished, I climbed in, facing him, our hands finding each other under the covers.

"So, tell me more about this marina deal," I said, wanting to prolong the night.

"I haven't figured anything out yet," Cal replied. "I just know in my gut this is the right thing to do. I want us to be independent again. Financially and emotionally."

"Money always comes with strings."

"Yeah. And family money more than most."

I drew circles on his palm. "Will you leaving the company be an issue?"

"Dad won't be happy. Mom will likely have things to say but no. There are immensely talented people who can step straight in. If anything, my leaving is a good thing."

"Will you miss this house?"

Cal didn't answer right away, his gaze distant

as he considered my question. "Not for the traditional reasons. Not because it holds good memories. But I'll miss this view."

Even I had to admit that we'd be hard-pressed to find a view quite this good.

"But a view doesn't make up for years of emptiness. I want our next house to be filled with memories like tonight."

"What, having sex on the rug?" I asked, amused.

"Yeah. But also being together and joking. Of dinners and painting and all the things I wish we'd had before."

I stopped tracing his palm and instead pressed mine to his. "Today was a good memory."

"Mm," he agreed. "The best."

"How quickly could they put it on the market?"

"Tomorrow, if I ask."

I nodded. "Then let's do it."

"You sure?"

"Completely." I glanced around. "This house will be perfect for someone. It's just that someone isn't us."

Cal laughed; the sound surprised.

"Well, fuck," he muttered, squeezing my hand. "Guess we're doing this."

"Hundred percent."

CHAPTER 9

Calvin

I signed the papers, then handed them over to Emily, exchanging a grin with her as we did.

"And that's it." The real estate agent stood, holding out a hand to me. "Congratulations."

I shook his hand, then watched him offer the same to Emily, feeling freer than I had in years.

"It's really done?" Emily clarified. It was early April, and she wore a light dress pink dress paired with a purple denim jacket and brown heels.

"It's really done," The agent confirmed, giving us both a nod.

"It's done," Emily whispered, looking up at me, her face aglow.

"Come here." I pulled her into me, pressing a kiss to her red-lipped mouth. "Silly."

"Not silly," she protested, pressing kisses back. "Just happy."

The white hell house had sold on Valentine's Day, and we'd moved into a rental while searching for a replacement. I'd resigned the week following our bedroom planning session, my parents having a conniption.

I'd finished in mid-February, then taken March off, Emily and I backpacking through Peru on our long overdue vacation. We'd returned home to search for a house while I started work at the marina. Em had decided that she would be going back to work as a music teacher whenever she found a position. In the meantime, she'd made it her full-time job to find us a house. Pity for her we'd found it after viewing only three.

We'd pulled up at the average beach cottage, the ramshackle weatherboard rough and worn, the garden overgrown. I'd heard her sharp intake of breath, then her hand had found mine, squeezing it tight.

As soon as we'd walked through the door, the sun streaming through the windows and glinting off the wooden floorboards, she'd turned to me, hands raised to her mouth.

"This is it," she'd said, her heart in her eyes. "This is our happy home."

It needed work. The roof needed replacing, and the damned garden had grown into the eaves in some places, but I'd agreed. It felt like ours.

The agent handed over the key. "Enjoy your new home, and don't hesitate to call if you need anything."

We took it and drove to the house, loaded with essentials. At the cottage, Emily leapt from the car and raced to the door, bouncing in place while she waited for me to come with the key. I slid it in, then turned, gesturing at her to do the honours.

She did, turning the key and throwing it open. Just as she was about to step inside, I grabbed her arm, pulling her back, then bent, catching her under the knees and tipping her back to carry her over the threshold.

"Ugh," I pretended to groan. "You're so heavy."

"Calvin!" she squealed, laughing and throwing her arms around my neck.

"Welcome home, wife."

I stopped in the doorway, kissing her and enjoying the taste of happiness on her lips.

"Cal," she whispered, pressing her forehead against mine. "Thank you for giving me this moment."

"Thank you, Pretty Eyes, for making life sweeter."

I let her slide down my body until her feet touched the floor. "Honey and Tristan are on their way. Collins and Nick, and Willodean will be by later. I asked them to bring pizza."

She sent me a smile. "With extra pepperoni? That's Honey's favourite."

Emily was trying to develop a relationship with my family, determined to repair old wounds and forge new bonds. I knew she'd achieve it because she had already won me over.

"I'll text them," I promised, letting her go.

Later that night, after we'd bid farewell to our family and friends, Em and I lay on the mattress in our bedroom, staring out the big double windows to the sea in the distance.

"Will you play for me, Pretty Eyes?" I asked, running my fingers over her back.

She pushed up, raising an eyebrow. "Now?"

I nodded, settling into the bed, folding my arms behind my head to watch her.

"Okay," she rolled out of bed, scrambling lazily to her feet and moving naked to the far side of the room and picking up her violin and bow.

I watched, enjoying the movement of her body as she got into place.

"Any requests?" she asked, bow poised.

"Surprise me."

She began to play, the notes pitch-perfect. I recognised the song immediately, *Time After Time*. My gut clenched as she closed her eyes, giving in to the music, tears falling gently down her cheeks as she played.

Just looking at her made my chest tight. Beautiful, stunning, glorious. All descriptors paled in comparison to the reality of Emily.

I pushed up as she continued, coming to sit on the edge of the bed, appreciating how far she'd come, how far we'd come to be here. Together.

She finished, and in the silence that followed, I stood, crossing to set aside her instrument and pull her into my arms. Her face pressed into my chest.

"Thank you," I whispered into her hair. "Thank you for that gift."

"I love you," she replied. "Thank you for giving me beautiful memories to replace those I've lost."

I cupped her jaw, tilting her head back to

look at me. "In the summer, we're getting remarried. Just you and me at the courthouse. We're starting this over the right way."

Her heart in her eyes, love on her lips, she spoke the only answer I'd accept.

"Yes."

EPILOGUE

Emily

"Cal? We're home," I called, dropping a net filled with soccer balls by the front door. Ahead of me Honey and Tristan's oldest, pulled my son along, tugging him down to our rumpus room.

"Cal?" I called, smiling as I listened to the cousin's bicker. "You hear?"

"In here," I heard him call. I waddled down the hall, heading to the back of the cottage. We'd finally bit the bullet this year and decided to build an addition to the back. The kids were getting older, and we just needed a little more space.

I rested a hand on my swollen stomach, feeling our surprise baby kick.

So much for the vasectomy.

I couldn't be mad, though. Our children were a gift (if not a little hyperactive), and I loved each of them with all my being.

Besides, Cal holding a baby in his big hands, Cal cuddling our kids, Cal doing anything slightly domestic was the best kind of porn.

I found him in the nursery – or what would be the nursery for baby number four.

"Oh," I whispered, stepping through and looking around.

Cal had designed each of our children's rooms. He'd said he couldn't design their first room, but he was determined to help with their second. I'd reminded him that I didn't have a say in what my uterus walls looked like, but he didn't seem to care. And each time, he'd surprised and delighted me with his choices – and this one was no different.

"Oh, Cal." I lifted a hand to my mouth, tears shimmering on my lashes.

The room featured a jungle theme, with animals peeking out from various areas. Cal had painted a large mural on one wall, and I could see where he'd allowed our other children to press their hands to the painting, creating a little plant out of their efforts.

"What do you think?" he asked, swinging an arm out. "Not too shabby."

"It's perfect," I answered, coming to his side and allowing him to pull me close. "Just perfect."

His hand dropped to my stomach. "Gotta be for our little monkey."

I heard a crash followed by laughter from the other room and sighed. "Speaking of little monkeys..."

"I got it, go put your feet up."

I did as instructed, settling into the rocking chair in the corner of the room near the crib and setting it to motion. My hands settled on my stomach, exhaustion suddenly setting in.

"You have the best daddy, little one. And your big brothers and sister are going to love you."

I must have dozed off because I next woke in my bed, Cal pressing a kiss to my forehead.

"Hungry?" he asked, voice soft.

"What time is it?"

"After eight."

"Eight?" I repeated, startled.

"Mm, don't worry. Your ratbags have been fed, watered and bathed. They even got two and a half stories before falling asleep."

He kissed my cheek, tenderly brushing strands away. "It appears that, for the moment, we're alone, wife."

I sighed, leaning into his touch and closing my eyes. "Tell me your good memory for today."

It was a question we'd gotten into the habit of asking each other over the years and now asked each other at the end of the day. A reminder that every moment was precious.

My memories had never returned, but that no longer mattered because Cal tried constantly to replace each one with something infinitely more precious – new, better memories.

"This moment is feeling like a winner," he replied, holding me.

"Mm, same."

He lifted my chin, his lips just brushing mine. "Thank you for the memory."

"Thank you for this moment. I love you."

"Love you too, Pretty Eyes."

I hope you loved Emily and Calvin.
This book turned out far more emotional than I anticipated, but I hope you saw a little piece of me and my journey in this story.
If you'd like more, check out the bonus slice of life on my website.

You can continue the entire series by checking them out on my website at www.EvieMitchell.com

*If you enter the code **EBOOK10** you can get 10% off your purchase from my website.*

ABOUT THE AUTHOR

Hey, I'm Evie Mitchell.
I'm a thirty-something romance author (she/her/hers) living with disability. I believe in inclusion, accessibility, and fierce romance. My loves include steamy romance novels, my sexy husband, our THREE sausage dogs (THE FUR!!!), and my ever-growing collection of book-related mugs.

As a woman with a diverse work history, including in areas such as hospitality, retail, emergency response, event management, human rights, disability access, and security— my books are filled with true stories (bridezillas), worst-case scenarios (malfunctioning zippers), and my favorite tropes (one-bed).

I'm a strong proponent of #OwnVoices, and specialize in fiercely inclusive happily ever afters.

EvieMitchell.com
Socials: @EvieMitchellAuthor

ALSO BY EVIE MITCHELL

All Access Series

Knot My Type

Love Flushed

Darn Knit All

Larsson Siblings

Thunder Thighs

Clean Sweep

The X-List

Reality Check

The Christmas Contract

The A-List

Capricorn Cove

The Shake-up

Double the D

Muffin Top

The Mrs. Clause

Double Breasted

As You Wish

You Sleigh Me

Meat Load

Resolution Revolution

Dogg Pack

Puppy Love

Bad English

The Frock Up

Pier Pressure

Trick or Trent

New Year's Faye

Reigning Hearts

The Marriage Claim

Silent Knight

Men of Trinity Bay

Kink in the Road

Nameless Souls MC

Runner

Wrath

Ghost

Shield

Elliot Security

Rough Edge

Bleeding Edge

www.ingramcontent.com/pod-product-compliance
Lightning Source LLC
Chambersburg PA
CBHW010021200726
48283CB00015B/3294